Chloe's Matchmaking Terrier

A MORNING LAKE NOVELLA
BOOK 1

LORRAINE PATON

DEDICATION

Thank you to my beautiful family and friends
for your continued support!
And thank you to everyone who has
read my stories, because of you
this has been an amazing and wonderful journey!

ACKNOWLEDGMENTS

First I must thank all the people who have read and enjoyed my books! You are awesome!

To my wonderful beta readers (Pati, Mahrie, and Darlene), my fabulous critique group (June, Deb and Sarah) and my patient editor: you have helped me so much by taking the time to read, offer comment and assist me with the preparation of this story. You are beautiful!

Thank you also to my family for sticking with me through this adventure. You are fabulous!

Thank you all for being a part of my journey.

~~~

And thank you to everyone who reads this book. I hope you enjoy Chloe and Luke's story!

~~~

PROLOGUE

(Author's note: This prologue was originally published in 2014 edition of Treasures Along the Fenceline *as a short story titled "Charlie's Idea.")*

Helen Trent leaned back in her rocking chair and looked across the countryside. People said these should be her golden years, but there wasn't much golden about the days lately, particularly since the chair beside her was empty now. Still, she didn't usually allow herself to feel the loneliness.

Today was the exception.

Charlie would have been teasing her by now, saying he had a special surprise for her. Her *surprise* was never a surprise, but it *was* the one day he kicked her out of the kitchen and made all the meals, including a chocolate cake complete with icing and candles. When Devin was a young boy, he'd help decorate with candies, usually in the misshapen form of whatever he was fascinated with at the time. One year it was a pirate made from licorice, followed by a dinosaur of mints the next, and then a series of horses and more horses.

Sure, the cake was from a box and the icing was the pre-made kind you found in the grocery store's bakery section, but it was the best damn cake she'd ever eaten.

The sun was crawling around the house now, inching toward where she sat in the shadowy confines of the porch, not that she needed shade on this early May day. She hugged her jacket closer over her body and nudged the rocking chair into motion.

She'd always thought he'd be there at her side, just as he had been most of her life.

And then he had to up and die.

Helen blinked away a stray tear, surprised she had any in her after all these years. She sat, rocked and allowed herself a moment to ponder what might have been.

Sunlight crept closer to her shaded perch. She watched it dispassionately as it covered one of her feet. Then the other. And still she rocked.

The warmth of the sun sent a shiver down her skin.

It was good that Devin had gone out of the house today—if he were here, he'd be trying to shoo her inside. He said he had to run errands, which she knew included picking up a cake from the bakery with the fancy icing roses.

The brightness continued to absorb her, climbing ever so slowly up her denim-covered legs. When it reached her hand, her fingers tingled as though the sunlight had a physical form. A presence.

Then the rocker beside her moved.

It was just a little wayward breeze that'd caught the chair just right, but for a moment she wanted to believe—pretend Charlie was there with her again, holding her hand.

She closed her eyes and let her chair move rhythmically while the warmth caressed the back of her hand.

She could hear him, knew what he'd say. "Nellie, you're not doing yourself any favors by sittin' out here in the cold."

She frowned. "I can do what I want, you old goat, and you know I will. So sit and talk to me for a minute." She let the imagined conversation play out in her mind's eye. The fantasy was a rare birthday present to herself.

He chuckled. "What do you want to talk about?"

"Surprise me."

They sat in silence for a bit. He'd always said he was never too good with words. "Why haven't you gone and tried to find another man?"

Helen shook her head. This was not the conversation she'd anticipated, but she kept her eyes firmly closed, imagining him sitting in the chair beside hers. "What the hell kind of question is that?"

He pinched her hand. "My mother never did understand how I could love a woman who could swear like you. She still doesn't."

Helen flinched. Charlie was talking as if his mother was alive, but she'd died before Devin was born, over thirty years ago. A strange impulse to open her eyes stole over her heart. Was Charlie really here with her? Was he visiting?

She didn't believe in that kind of thing. Even when they did that on her daytime TV shows, she always berated the writers for not coming up with something a little more original. But Charlie wasn't acting like himself ... But at the same time he was.

Was he a ghost?

He'd asked her a question and she decided to answer. "I don't have time for another man."

"You're a woman who needs lovin', Nellie." The timbre of his voice deepened, the way it always did when he used to suggest they retire early in the evening.

She didn't have to look in a mirror to know she was blushing. The man could do that to her in just a few words. And she loved him for it. "There'll never be another, and you well know it."

He sighed. "I want you to be happy."

"I'd be happy if that son of ours quit pining over Livy. She wasn't good for him when she was alive, and she certainly isn't good for him now that she's dead." She clenched her fist. "I want him to be happy. That's what would make me happy."

He patted her hand. "No meddling, remember? We agreed there'd be no meddling."

"I haven't done a thing and he's sinking deeper into that rut of his."

"We weren't talking about Devin," Charlie said. "This is about you. Your happiness."

"You still don't listen to me," she said, but there was no anger in her words.

"Don't you wish you could spread out all that love of yours? I can share you for a spell, if you want. You know that, right? I'll be waiting for you, no matter what."

Helen's heart raced as the seed of a plan came to life. It was spring, a time for new things. "Oh, Charlie! That's a great idea!"

He blinked at her. "Now why do I think you're gonna twist my words around and tell me two plus two makes twenty five?"

"Shouldn't the next generation have the chance to experience the love we did?" She hadn't been so excited in years. "There are so many lonely people in this little sleepy town ..."

"Didn't we talk about meddling a minute ago?" He squeezed her hand. "Don't you remember what people used to say about your crazy Aunt Harriet?"

"She's the one who introduced us. And I wouldn't have gone to the dance with you without a little encouragement from my *crazy* aunt. You should be thanking her, if you see her around."

He shook his head, but his grin was enough for her to know he was onboard with her plan. "You're about as subtle as that old Clydesdale your dad used to own."

Helen straightened. "Never you mind about my methods. It's the end that'll be important, and we both know it."

"So what's your plan?" He was indulging her, but that was okay.

"I think I'll have to make it up as I go along." Helen tapped her chin with her free hand. "I don't see a good candidate for Devin yet, so maybe I need to practice on someone in the meantime ... Hone my skills. A roper doesn't catch a calf his first time out."

"There's more of Harriet in you than I'd imagined."

Helen glanced toward him, in her mind's eye. He leaned back in the rocking chair, with his denim jacket hanging open and loose over his favorite blue shirt. His jeans were the ones with the hole in the knee and his boots were his working ones, so they were covered with enough scuffs and horse shit it was hard to imagine what they'd looked like new. But it wasn't what he was wearing that drew her breath away—it was the way the sunlight was catching on the stubble on his cheek, the glint in his eye, and the grin breaking over his mouth. "You are as handsome as ever, you old devil."

"And you're still my best girl."

"I love you, Charlie. I've missed you." She swallowed. "I don't want you to leave."

"Darlin', I'm always with you. And I'm always lovin' you—"

Charlie faded. She opened her eyes, hoping to catch another fleeting glimpse of him. A shadowy figure blocked the sunlight from hitting her hand.

"Mom?"

Helen blinked. "Devin?" She cleared her throat. "What's the matter?"

"You fell asleep out here, though I don't know how. It's freezing."

Helen glanced down at her hand, the one Charlie had been holding. It was warm. And it still tingled. She smiled up at her son. "I've just been given the best idea!"

"Given?" He raised one eyebrow at her statement, and he peered around as if looking for another person on the empty porch. "What idea?"

"You'll see ..." Helen smiled.

CHAPTER 1

Ginger, the youthful and energetic Airedale Terrier that she was, yanked on the nylon leash and headed for the overgrown ditch by the side of the road.

"Good grief, not again." Chloe tried to resist the tug. A few months ago Chloe Wagner would never have been awake early enough to see dew, and now, after diving into the ditch more times than she could count, her sneakers were soaked with it. It shouldn't be this hard to walk a dog. And it didn't help her mood that the sharp edges of the crushed gravel stabbed through the thin soles of her shoes or that her arm ached from trying to control her new foster puppy.

"Get up here this instant," Chloe growled and much to her surprise, Ginger paused, cocked her head and glanced over her shoulder. The dog plodded up to the top of the ditch and wagged her tail. Who knew? The same tone her mother had used to reprimand her as a child worked on terriers, too.

When the roar of an engine warned of someone's approach, Chloe grabbed Ginger's leash tighter, reeling the dog in until she could grab her collar. Chloe shuffled farther to the side of the road, praying Ginger wouldn't take it as an invitation to investigate the ditch again. The old-style pickup sped toward them. Small pebbles spewed into the air, clattering against the underside of the truck as it slowed on its approach to them.

The vehicle sputtered to a halt directly beside them, and the dust cloud trailing behind was caught by a little breeze going the other direction.

The window was cranked down, and blaring country music escaped into the quiet of the roadside. A smiling gray-haired woman leaned out and greeted her.

"Mrs. Trent, what a surprise. Do you live out here?" Chloe said. Helen Trent was a third cousin through marriage or something or other, a fact Chloe had discovered at a family reunion two years earlier. It wasn't a close connection, but family was still family. With her parents having moved to Edmonton after she graduated, Chloe didn't have many familial connections in Morning Lake anymore.

"Yep, up the way." The older woman cranked her thumb back and pointed with it over her shoulder. Chloe supposed she should have known that, since she had a vague memory of Helen's son Devin holding a house party in high school, but he was a few years older than she was and she'd only been there once. "You should really call me Helen, like I told you the last time I saw you."

Ah, yes, the family reunion. The venue, a rustic campground in the heart of Banff National Park, had been amazing. The memories were not. Christopher had whacked her piece of her parents' anniversary cake out of her hand and it'd landed on her Auntie Jean's straw hat. *You promised me you were watching your diet* was his only explanation.

"Are you renting the old Lovecraft place?"

Chloe nodded. "I moved in last week. Two of the pharmacists at Jefferson's Drug Mart are taking maternity leaves, which overlap by about five months." Chloe shrugged. "Since I recently decided it was time to leave my last place, this temporary position is perfect for me."

"That's a good thing—those maternity leaves—that the government does." Helen nodded. Then she cocked her head to the side. "Wait, didn't you work for that *friend* of yours?"

Chloe swallowed. Sweat pricked through her skin. "Christopher? Yes." She took a deep breath and smiled. "I loved the people who came into the store, but it was time to move on." Her voice wasn't as steady as she'd like. She'd worked at Christopher's store since she'd graduated from university, and it had been harder to say good-bye to her regular customers than to the man she'd thought she'd marry.

"So your friend? He didn't come?"

She shuddered. "Ah, no."

Helen hooted. "Well, thank heavens."

Chloe laughed, relieved at Helen's unexpected reaction. For so long, she'd thought Christopher had the right of things. It'd been unnerving to finally walk away. She was proud that she had, but she'd worried about what people would think of the fat girl who left the handsome, successful business owner—

Nope, she wasn't thinking that way anymore. She straightened her shoulders and reiterated her personal mantra. "He decided my waist was too thick, and I decided his head was too thick."

Shit, she shouldn't have said that aloud, especially in front of one of the most well-connected women in Morning Lake. How long would it take for everyone in town to know about her less-than-amicable breakup?

"Good girl." Helen grinned. Then she waved her hand through the air. "I'm glad you tossed his scrawny ass to the door, particularly if he couldn't appreciate your figure. You're curvy, just like I used to be when I was your age. And believe me—" Helen winked, "— a good man appreciates those bits. Those skinny girls wish they had hourglass figures."

Hourglass. Yep, that was her—top *and* bottom heavy.

Ginger whined at her feet, breaking through her thoughts. Right, Ginger was going to help her get fit. If Chloe had only herself to consider, she would succumb to her lazy self's rationale for sitting on the couch, but if she were accountable to an energetic puppy that needed regular exercise, then she would have to go out. Much better than the damned treadmill Christopher had given her on her last birthday. She could hardly wait to shed the weight her *own way* and sashay into his store in a slinky red dress. Ha! Wouldn't he be surprised?

"Now, who is this little one?" Helen smiled at the dog.

Chloe glanced down at her companion, who was now sniffing her foot. "This is Ginger. She was returned to Laura's kennel two months after being adopted. Isn't that sad? I'm fostering her until another interested family comes to adopt her permanently, but Laura doesn't think that'll happen any time soon. The last puppy she fostered out never got adopted because everyone thought there was something wrong with a puppy who got returned."

"What a sweet looking dog. Maybe bit feisty, hey?"

"Feisty, yes, that's one word for it." *Stubborn* also came to mind.

Helen adjusted her rear-view mirror. "You weren't walking up to those trees, were you?"

"We were, but it'll have to wait until tomorrow." She glanced at the screen on her cell phone. "I start work in an hour."

"You don't want to go up there." Helen shook her head. "A coyote family dens there. Bad business for you and your puppy."

"Oh, I didn't know." Chloe surveyed the land. She'd always lived in town, so she didn't really know much about wild animals or where they lived. "I guess we could walk to the wetland—"

"Oh, no. Don't go that way. I've seen a badger up there. Fierce creatures, them. Have you seen the claws on them?" Helen curled her fingers and swiped them through the air.

"Oh, that doesn't sound good."

"No, it isn't."

If Chloe didn't know better, she would think Helen winked at her again as she nodded to the south. But that didn't make any sense. "Thanks for the warnings," Chloe said.

"Any time, my dear." Helen grinned. "And who knows, maybe by the end of the summer you might decide to stick around."

"Oh, I—"

"Anyway, I'll be into your store later this morning. I have to get my arthritis medication." She wiggled her thick fingers. "Some days it ..." The older woman shook her head.

Chloe made a mental note to check on Helen's prescriptions first thing. One part of her job was to monitor her clients' responses to the drug therapy. If Helen's current medication wasn't working, she might be able to recommend some alternatives.

After Helen left, Chloe considered her walking route options while leading Ginger back home. Her rental house was at the end of a dead-end road. When she walked up the road to the nearest intersection, she had three directions from which to choose. Helen had just eliminated two roads from her route, which left only one last road to the south.

Chloe bit her lip when she turned in that direction. Yep, there was Luke Larsen's place. The road went straight by his house—at least it used to be Luke's when they were teenagers. She wasn't sure if he'd taken over the ranch from his parents or not. Maybe they had even sold the place.

Was that what Helen had winked about? No, it couldn't be.

A dense caragana hedge and a row of tall cottonwoods shielded Luke's two-story house from Chloe's immediate view, but she could picture it exactly as it had been on prom night,when a big group of them met there for graduation photos. They were all in their gowns and tuxedos, imagining so many great adventures ahead. His mother had the prettiest flowers in her garden, so it had been an obvious choice for the photo session. The pictures turned out beautifully, but every time she thumbed through those photos, her heart felt pinched in her chest.

Luke was the guy every girl's father wanted her to date: kind, considerate, and polite. And he was the guy every girl's mother wanted her to date: cute, sweet, and funny. But when a girl's parents wanted her to date a boy, that was the last boy a girl wanted to date.

She had few regrets in her life. Her decision to live with Christopher was an obvious one. And her decision to *not* date Luke was another. After all these years, he still invaded her thoughts more than he should.

She could only hope he didn't live there anymore, because she had no idea what she would say to him.

CHAPTER 2

The next morning

Luke looked out the window and spit his cereal across the breakfast table.

Sonofabitch. If it wasn't his high school wet dream, Chloe, waltzing across his view. Okay, she wasn't so much waltzing as being dragged by an orange dog. He watched her, not quite believing his eyes, as she passed by his house. At this distance, she was as beautiful and curvy as he remembered and he bet she was just as smart and sweet now as she had been back in the day. But it still wasn't what he expected at six a.m. in the middle of the bald-assed prairie.

He had heard someone had rented the house a mile up the way. Could that have been her?

Luke grabbed a dishtowel from the counter and mopped up the milk and cereal, feeling a helluva lot more optimistic about the season ahead than he had for a long time.

His sister said he was too much of a romantic, which was ridiculous. Larsen men weren't romantic. He was a normal man who wanted a wife and a family. That wasn't romantic; it was, well, a wish any normal man would have.

What if she wasn't single? Luke tempered his hope.

A few minutes later, after he'd poured his coffee into a go-cup and was about to pull on his boots, Jasper, his old dog, started barking again. He walked to the window, hoping Chloe had returned.

And there she was.

She must have turned around at the intersection.

She did not so much as glance his way, or she would have seen him standing in his big window. It was almost as if he was in high school again, hoping she would look at him when she passed by his locker. Back then, she always did. She'd flash a smile, and he'd be ruined for his next class.

God, she was still beautiful.

Even the way her long dark hair was pulled back in a ponytail was attractive, bouncing with each step she took. She had tied her jacket around her waist, revealing a tight T-shirt underneath. Shit. She had curves and softness in all the right places. How was he supposed to think about going to work when she was outside his driveway wearing that?

He stumbled to the door and was halfway down the yard in his socks before he knew what he was doing. He didn't have a plan, but he couldn't let this opportunity slide by the way he had in high school.

"Hey, stranger," he called to her.

***

Chloe spun toward the man calling to her. Her heart galloped. He had only said two words, but she had known his voice immediately.

To say Luke Larsen had aged well was an understatement. He was lean, tanned and sexy as hell.

Her breath caught, and she forgot for a moment what she had been doing. Then Ginger rushed toward him, jolting Chloe forward, propelling her to the man she wished she had dated ten years earlier.

"Luke," she said, wishing she had not sounded quite so breathless at the mere sight of him. "How are you? It's been a long time. I didn't know you still lived here." Could she have spoken any faster?

"My parents bought a condo in town a few years back and signed this place over to us kids." He shrugged. "Sandy's already got a place with her husband, so they decided I should live here. Mom almost changed her mind when I sodded over her flower beds." He glanced over at the area where the daylilies and hollyhocks had once lived, and shrugged.

Chloe smiled and shook her head. "I don't blame her. Her garden was legendary."

Luke grinned and Chloe's insides melted. Ginger leaned against her leg. Thankful for the distraction, Chloe patted her dog's head. She glanced down. "You aren't wearing shoes."

"I wanted to catch you before you disappeared down the road." Luke laughed and winked at her.

Her stomach fluttered and heat rose to her cheeks. Luke could be dangerous for her heart. "How is your sister? I haven't seen her in ... Well, I suppose I haven't seen either of you in years."

"She's good. She and John have a boy and girl, and almost every animal a person could imagine."

"She always was bringing home orphans, wasn't she?" Chloe laughed. "And you?"

"Not too much to report other than taking over the homestead. You?"

He was single.

Chloe swallowed, wishing she could swallow down her sudden

excitement at that bit of news. If only she had worn something more attractive than an old T-shirt and a pair of jeans. She prayed her jacket at her waist was at least hiding her muffin-top. She yanked it down, and Luke's eyes followed her movement.

"I ..." Chloe hesitated. She didn't want to talk to Luke about Christopher, so she concentrated on the positive things that had happened in her life. "I'm a pharmacist now, and I'm here for the summer working at Jefferson's Drug Mart."

"And who is this?" Luke crouched down and scratched Ginger behind the ears. The fur ball had no pride, letting her tongue loll about her mouth at his touch, leaning into his hand for more.

When Chloe left a few minutes later, she had to drag Ginger away, but she didn't blame the dog. Not one little bit.

CHAPTER 3

Within a day, Luke had heard the rumors about Chloe. His sister had said she was here to nurse a broken heart, but she didn't seem as if she was pining for anyone—not when she had smiled and blushed at him the way she had. Besides, if Helen Trent, who had tracked him down at the post office, was to be believed, Chloe was damn lucky to get rid of the jerk.

He couldn't shake the thought that Chloe needed a real man, someone who would appreciate her. Someone like him.

The next morning when he saw her on the road, he intercepted her again.

"You have your shoes on today," Chloe teased.

He grinned and tipped his cowboy hat to her.

Ginger jumped against his leg.

"Ginger, stop," Chloe begged as she tugged the dog's collar.

Luke looked at the Airedale, whose tail wagged at his attention. "Down," he said in a firm voice and the dog sat.

Chloe gaped. "How did you do that?"

Luke shrugged. "I've been around animals my whole life. I guess that counts for something."

Chloe blinked at her dog, who was still seated and staring at Luke.

"Could you teach me how to do that?"

Luke nodded—now here was a perfect opportunity to spend more time with Chloe. Maybe he could win her over through her dog. "Absolutely."

By the weekend, they had covered such basics as "sit" and "stay," but Ginger only obeyed Chloe when she felt like it. At least Chloe seemed to be enjoying herself, even today as they sat on his front lawn and played with the dogs. Things had quickly become easy between Chloe and him. It was as if she hadn't left.

Luke lobbed the tennis ball for the umpteenth time, and Ginger and Jasper sprinted after it. Jasper's chase was more like a lumbering tag-along, but the poor dog was getting up there in age. Ginger grabbed the ball out of the air after a bounce, and raced back. She was panting hard, and drool dripped from her jaw. When she dropped the slobber-covered ball, Chloe groaned.

"Eww," she said. "That's disgusting."

He laughed as he picked it up. "Look how happy she is. It's worth it." As if to prove his point, Ginger bounced at his feet, her attention never leaving the ball in his hand. When he let it loose, she bolted. Jasper barked twice, then plopped down by Chloe on the grass.

"I guess," Chloe said. She scratched Jasper behind his ears and watched Ginger grab the ball. The dog deposited it beside Luke's foot again. Her mouth hung open with heavy breathing.

"Okay, sweetheart, that's enough for now." Luke patted Ginger. The dog circled for a few minutes, before toddling off to get some water from the bucket he'd left at the front step. Luke washed his hands under the outdoor tap and wiped them on his jeans. Then he returned to lie back on the grass beside Chloe. "I can't remember the last time I did this."

"What?" She turned toward him. Their faces were close enough that he could almost kiss her.

"Hung out, tossed a ball, you name it." His voice was quieter than normal, as if some part of his brain was trying to weave an air of intimacy between them. She smiled. He put his hands under his head and crossed his feet to keep his limbs to himself. Small, bright white clouds dotted the deep blue sky. He took a breath and couldn't believe how relaxing this was. Or how comfortable he could be with Chloe after such a short amount of time.

Chloe stretched out beside him. "Huh, me too, I guess. Do you have things to do? No, that's a stupid question. You probably have a huge to-do list."

"Nothing that can't wait a bit." There were always jobs to do on the ranch, but at this moment he couldn't think of a damned thing. The cattle were in the pasture, the fields were sown, and that seemed like enough. He squinted at the plane flying overhead. As a kid he'd tried to guess what type of plane it was; now his nephew said there was an app to tell you which planes were in your area. It didn't seem like as much fun.

"Do you like it?" Chloe sat up, braced herself on one arm, and looked down at him.

"What?"

"Living here, working with horses and cattle every day, all that." She waved her hand through the air.

What could he tell her? He'd wondered that very thing for the last few years. His days were filled with work, or thoughts about work. There was that old cliché everyone liked to toss around about loving what you do, but he didn't believe it. Not now. He *did* love what he did, but it wasn't enough. He wanted a family. He wanted a woman he could share his life with. And he'd been wondering if it'd be possible to find someone he could love who would want to share this life with him.

He opted for the best answer he could muster at a moment's notice. "I can't imagine doing anything else." He glanced in her direction to gauge her reaction. She was nodding.

"I know what you mean," she said. "I love being a pharmacist, helping people live happier lives, getting to know the people who come in ... All of it." She smiled at him. "I can't imagine doing anything else either."

It was true. He'd seen her at the store, chatting with customers. She was genuine and attentive with them, and he admired how she took the time to talk to them and answer their questions. He'd waited for nearly half an hour to take her to coffee while she answered Mrs. Stapleton's queries, making sure the older woman understood everything. Sure, it was part of Chloe's job, but anyone who saw her would know she enjoyed it and wanted to help. She'd always been like that. It was one of the reasons he'd fallen for her in high school, and it was one of the reasons he was falling for her all over again.

"I guess Ginger and I should get back to the house," Chloe said.

"Hey, do you want to go to the lake next weekend?"

Chloe blinked. "Go swimming?" She glanced down at her body and tugged at her shirt.

Shit. That was the wrong thing to ask, wasn't it? Given what Helen had said about Chloe's ex and his mistaken thoughts about her sexy body, Luke should have known better. His sister and mother were self-conscious about their bodies, too, and they hadn't been humiliated by their husbands.

"We don't have to go swimming," he said quickly. "We could take the boat out on the water."

Chloe swallowed. "Let me think about it, okay? I'm not sure what my work schedule is for next weekend."

Luke nodded. He stood up and reached for her.

Chloe placed her hands in his, and he stroked his thumbs over her smooth skin. She looked up at him, and he wanted to try to convince her to stay a little longer. When he helped her to her feet, she fell against him. Her soft curves brushed his body. Her eyes flashed and she licked her lips.

He leaned down, eager to feel her mouth beneath his.

She stepped back ... and he let her go.

Chloe was only here for the summer, a temporary position. And then what? She would have to move to some other drug store in some other town. As their class valedictorian, she'd always been smart as hell and destined for bigger places than Morning Lake. That was part of the reason he'd never had the guts to ask her out. His destiny was right here. It wasn't as if he could relocate his land. But even knowing that, he wanted to spend more time with her.

And that was a frightening realization, because he wasn't sure a summer with Chloe would be enough.

CHAPTER 4

A hot streak hit Morning Lake earlier than normal. The heat was smothering when you were in a house with no air conditioner. Maybe she should go to the lake with Luke.

The idea made all kinds of images pop up in her mind. And, if possible, her body heated up even more. They'd been spending a lot of time together and he'd asked her to the lake, so what did that mean? And had he been about to kiss her?

No. She shook her head. She'd been imagining things.

She didn't have time to think about that. She was already running late because an electrical storm had knocked out her power in the middle of the night, resetting her alarm clock. She'd slept in and now the heat of the day was on them. Chloe sighed and studied Ginger, who was sprawled beneath the shade of a tree.

"Come on, Ginger," Chloe said, "let's go for a walk."

Ginger eyed Chloe for a second, then put her head back down again. Usually Ginger was determined to spend time at Luke's, so this sudden apathy was telling. The poor dog was suffering in the heat as much as she was. Maybe they didn't need to walk today—

No, she couldn't make excuses. She'd made a commitment.

"I'm working the late shift so we can't walk when I get home." She looked up at the sky. "And now I'm reasoning with a dog."

Chloe walked to Ginger and rubbed her belly for a minute before snapping the leash on her collar. "Let's go."

Ginger padded beside her down the road without her usual enthusiasm. They had already passed the corner and were nearly at Luke's place, when he pulled up beside them in his truck. At Luke's arrival, Ginger wagged her tail so hard she almost lost her balance.

"Want a lift?"

Ginger whimpered with happiness.

"No, we're good." Chloe smiled.

"See you in a few," he said. Then he drove toward his house.

Should she be worried that things had become too natural between them? He didn't even seem to question if she'd stop. It was very neighborly.

Just like her dad had always said, Luke was a good guy.

That was all.

Ginger pulled Chloe faster down the road now, a spurt of energy hitting her after seeing Luke. The girl had no dignity. It was all she could do to deliver Chloe to him as quickly as possible, a matchmaker in matted fur.

When they arrived at Luke's place, he had his arms full of groceries. She hovered at the driveway. In all the time they'd spent together, she hadn't actually been up to his house yet. He indicated with his head that she should come over. She hesitated, but Ginger didn't need another invitation.

Chloe climbed the stairs to his door, wondering with each step what she was doing. His door was open. Should she walk in?

She opted for a lawn chair in the shade of his covered porch instead.

A moment later, he came out with a bucket of water. "I meant to be finished with the groceries by the time you got here, but Odie, my cat, brought home a mouse for me. I remember how squeamish you were in Biology when we had to do dissections, so I thought I should clean it up first."

"After surviving all my university classes, I'm much better now." She laughed, but she was touched that he'd remembered.

Then Luke turned to Ginger. "Sit."

Ginger immediately plopped down on her butt.

"I don't believe it." Chloe rolled her eyes. "Why does she still listen to you better than me?" Ginger never listened to her. Thinking about what Luke had already taught her, Chloe could only surmise that Ginger recognized him as the alpha in her pack.

A pack meant they were family. Chloe swallowed.

Luke winked at Chloe, but praised the dog. "There you go, sweetheart," he said as he placed the container on the wooden planks for Ginger. The dog dove at the water.

And was that really a pang of jealousy she felt over the fact he'd called her dog *sweetheart* instead of her?

No, people couldn't be jealous of animals. Specifically, she wasn't jealous of her dog's relationship with Luke.

"I'll be back in a minute," he said to her.

His big dog Jasper emerged from the house and immediately went to Ginger. They sniffed one another, and Ginger acknowledged the other dog's superiority by dropping her head a little.

Chloe laughed. A few weeks ago she wouldn't have realized what the dogs were doing. It appeared Luke wasn't just teaching Ginger.

Chloe leaned back in the chair, wondering why his porch was so much cooler and more comfortable than hers. She lifted her hair up from her back, and perspiration trickled down her neck.

It was bad enough that she was out in the T-shirt Christopher had declared a disgrace since it showed every bump and bulge, but now she was coated in sweat, too. And it wouldn't help that she was sitting, making all the fat that wasn't delegated to her boobs and her butt compress into a lump.

She took a deep breath, and hugged her arms around her fat.

Luke emerged from the house with a big grin on his face as he carried out two vanilla ice cream cones. He presented one to her.

"I bought the ice cream for my niece and nephew, but on a day like today, who can resist?"

She studied the calorie-laden treat. Luke's eyes narrowed, as if he was aware of her internal struggle. "I don't know ..."

"Don't tell me you are on that weird diet my sister is trying," Luke said. She shifted uncomfortably. Then he looked her up and down, and she froze. Her skin flushed as if he'd physically touched her. "Believe me, you are perfect the way you are." His voice was deeper, and her body shuddered in response.

"Ah, thank you," she said. Of course he was just being sweet. But he raised an important point: Why shouldn't she enjoy her summer with a little ice cream? "And yes, I would love the ice cream."

He sat on the chair beside hers and they stared out at the quiet ranch.

The frozen treat melted quickly in the heat, and she licked the creamy drips with a happiness she hadn't experienced in years. When was the last time she'd eaten an ice cream cone without feeling Christopher's scorn? "Oh, my God." She moaned. "This is perfect."

She smiled at Luke, who, although he was eating his own treat, seemed transfixed on hers.

"What's up?" she asked.

He blinked, pulling his gaze up to hers. "You have a bit of ..." He leaned over and brushed her cheek. His touch was feather-light and yet there was no mistaking that he'd touched her. Then he licked his finger. "Just a bit of ice cream."

"Um ... Ah ... Thank you." She had no idea she could feel any hotter than she had a moment ago, but a sudden flush of heat shot over her skin.

"Yours is dripping! Lick!" He laughed. "Shit, so is mine!" Then he drew his tongue in a wide sweep over the melting mound atop the cone.

Her mind fell into the gutter for one agonizing second.

Then she finished her ice cream.

***

"Can't I drive you home?" Luke said, eager to stretch out all the time he had with her.

"Nah, we're good." Chloe shook her head, sending her hair fluttering over her shoulders.

His fingers twitched. He wished he could touch it, touch her.

"Ginger needs her exercise."

It didn't take a genius to figure out Chloe was really referring to herself needing exercise, but he let it go for now. That bastard she used to live with had done quite a number on her self-esteem. What he wouldn't give to teach him a few lessons of his own ...

More importantly, how could he help her to see how beautiful she was?

He scratched Ginger's head in farewell. Chloe waited beside them. When he stood, he could have her in his arms within one step. What would Chloe do if he kissed her?

God, she'd just arrived back in Morning Lake and he'd fallen for her as hard or harder than he had through twelve years of school. The memories of her licking that ice cream cone alone were going to haunt his nights for the rest of his life.

He lingered on his porch, watching her walk down the driveway and turn onto the road.

The sway of her sweet hips had him mesmerized.

Damn, he had it bad.

He waited until she'd disappeared behind his hedge before he forced himself to get up and go inside. He had to finish putting away his groceries before everything was ruined anyway.

The door hadn't closed behind him when a truck passed in front of his house.

Then her scream shattered the air.

CHAPTER 5

It was weird how he took in the billow of dust, the fading rumble of an engine, and the sweet smell of some flowering shrub as he raced across the yard to where Chloe had disappeared beyond his hedge. His heart thudded as he ran through possible explanations for why she'd screamed.

None of them were good.

The 100 yards to the end of the driveway lasted as long as a marathon. Finally he found her kneeling on the ground.

When she turned to him, he saw blood on her shirt. Air flew from his lungs, as though he'd been punched in the gut. "Chloe, shit. You're hurt."

"I'm okay, but ..." Her words ended on a ragged breath. Thank God she was okay.

When he knelt beside them, he discovered Ginger was still, too still. A gash at her head was bleeding, flowing through her thick fur and into the dry dirt. His heart hammered in his chest as he tried to assess if Ginger was already gone. Then she whimpered and lifted her paw.

He let out a deep breath. "Hold your hand over her cut. I'll get the truck."

Chloe's eyes were filled with tears. He squeezed her shoulder quickly before sprinting across the yard again. He stopped in the house long enough to grab a clean towel and then he hopped in his truck.

When he arrived at the end of the driveway, Chloe was attempting to lift the terrier, but the dog's limp body was too much for her to manage in her distraught state. Her gaze darted to Luke. The panic was unmistakable. He jumped out and ran to her side.

"Come on, Ginger, come on," Chloe chanted. "You'll be okay."

His heart broke listening to her, but he nudged her away from the dog so he could wrap the dog's head in the towel. As he gently lifted Ginger from the ground, she blinked but didn't fuss or nip.

Chloe hovered beside him, rubbing her blood-coated hands on her shorts. Luke didn't think she even realized what she was doing. He nodded to the door of the truck, and Chloe jumped up and opened it.

He lowered Ginger to the bench seat, thankful that his rebuilt pickup didn't have bucket seats. Chloe climbed into the cab, but there wasn't room

19

for her on the seat, too.

"I'm going with you. And don't tell me I can't because there is no room. I'll make do."

"You aren't sitting on the floor." It was one thing to rush the dog to the veterinary hospital, but what if something happened? He couldn't allow Chloe to endanger herself.

Chloe's hands formed into fists. "We're wasting time. We have to go."

Luke shook his head. "Get on the seat." Chloe looked ready to argue more, but his scowl silenced her. "I'll shift Ginger so her head is on your lap."

He leaned into the truck and lifted Ginger again, while Chloe clambered to the middle space. He insisted she fasten the seat belt before he lowered the dog to her lap. Chloe cradled the terrier's head, stroking the thick fur. Her sloped shoulders and wet cheeks were the picture of misery.

Luke swallowed. He'd been on the ranch long enough to see his fair share of death, but Chloe hadn't. He wanted to comfort her, offer her some reassurance, but he couldn't think of what to say. He couldn't promise that Ginger would be okay, because he didn't know.

At least he could deliver them safely to the pet hospital.

After five minutes of listening to Chloe's soft, unintelligible murmurs to Ginger, Luke needed to hear her speak to him. "What happened, Chloe?"

"There was a truck on the road. A big one like they have in the fields. And when it passed by, a rock flew out from its tires." Her voice was low, monotone. "Do you think she'll be okay?"

Luke cleared his throat. He still couldn't lie. "I don't know."

She took a ragged breath and returned to murmuring to Ginger.

CHAPTER 6

Five hours later, Luke was fighting the urge to pace, when the vet, Jeff Scott, joined them in the otherwise empty waiting room. Luke had been one of the first people in the community to go to him after Doc Grover left. They'd become friends; Luke trusted him and knew Jeff was a helluva good vet.

Jeff wiped his hands on a white towel and had a serious look on his face. That didn't seem promising. Luke tightened his hand on Chloe's. They'd said very little to one another for the time they'd been waiting, but he'd held her hand through it all, even when she'd called work to say she couldn't come in.

"Hey, Luke, Chloe," Jeff said as he pulled a chair toward them, then sat down. "Ginger's stable for now. I've stitched her up, but due to the type of injury I want to keep her overnight. She's sedated now, but when that wears off we'll have a better idea if there is any motor damage. I need to see her walk, how she holds her head, and do a few tests."

Chloe sucked in a deep breath and loosened her hand on Luke's. When she withdrew her heat, he wanted to grab it back. "That doesn't sound good. Is she going to be okay?"

"I've done what I can for her for now, but I'll know more in the morning."

"I understand." Chloe sniffled. "Can I see her before we go?"

"She's sedated—"

"I still want to." Chloe crossed her arms.

Jeff nodded and led them to a room at the back of the clinic. Ginger was sprawled across the floor of a clean crate. A plastic cone surrounded her head. Although the wound itself was covered in gauze, the area had been shaved. Given the length of the bandage, Luke imagined a nasty thick row of stitches under the covering.

Chloe opened the crate's door and stroked Ginger's fur. The terrier was still, but for the steady rise and fall of her chest. Chloe knelt and murmured in the dog's ear. She wiped a tear away and then closed the door again.

He'd never felt so useless. All he could do was guide her to the truck and drive her home.

They rode in silence. Luke searched his brain for something to say to comfort her, but nothing seemed right. When he pulled into her driveway, Chloe stayed in her seat.

"Do you want me to come in with you?" he asked.

She drew in a raspy breath and nodded. He followed her into the house.

They had washed up at the clinic, but their clothes were still stained with blood. Luke's shirt was hardened, and he could only imagine what Chloe's clothing was like. "Why don't you go clean up? I'll wait here."

"Thank you." She smiled weakly at Luke and he felt like a hero.

His T-shirt was black, so the blood didn't show much, but it was still there. When she left the room, he removed his shirt and tossed it in the kitchen garbage. Then he took some paper towels and washed the blood off in the kitchen sink. Luckily the night was as hot as the afternoon had been and he didn't miss the shirt.

When he heard the shower run, his mind clogged with what she'd look like with the water streaming over her luscious body. He swallowed. The shower kept running and running—like a sweet invitation. No, that wasn't what Chloe needed right now. He had to keep himself busy.

He paced around the room and came up with a plan.

When Chloe finally came back out, she stared at his chest. "What happened to your shirt?"

"I tossed it. I don't need it tonight anyway," he said.

She swallowed. Her eyes traveled over his body and he couldn't deny the pleasure he got from watching her look at him. He thought about flexing—who wouldn't?—but he refrained. Tonight wasn't about him. It was about Chloe and Ginger.

She went to the garbage and yanked the shirt out. The bloody paper towels tumbled out with it. "I'll wash it. I'll—"

"Chloe, leave it. It's just an old rag."

He crossed to her and took it from her hand. He wadded it into a ball, gathered the paper towels, and dropped them all in the pail again. "It's okay."

She eyed the shirt one last time and then nodded.

"You know what, I think I have a shirt in the truck. I'll be right back." He didn't usually carry a change of clothing, but he'd dressed in layers just a month ago when the mornings were still crisp. If he remembered correctly, he hadn't taken one of the shirts into the house yet. When he got to his truck, he called his brother-in-law to ask him to take care of his evening chores and check in on Jasper and Odie.

Luke figured he'd get a call from his sister first thing in the morning, asking about Chloe and why he was staying with her, even though he'd explained things to John.

When he returned a minute later, he found Chloe in the kitchen, right where he'd left her. Her gaze followed the path of his fingers as he buttoned his shirt. Her face flushed.

"Now, come here," Luke said. He led her to the couch, which appeared more comfortable than the awful wooden chairs at the table. He was pretty sure those were cheap garage sale finds. "I hope you don't mind, but I dug through your fridge and made some sandwiches."

"Oh, you didn't have to do that. I could have made them." She glanced awkwardly toward her kitchen, as if thinking about jumping up and re-making the meal.

"It's already done. You haven't eaten for hours." He placed a sandwich in her hand. "Here."

"I'm not hungry."

"Please. For me?"

He took a sandwich himself and sat down beside her.

She stared at the plate on the table. "I can't put food on the coffee table anymore. Ginger thinks it's hers." Chloe tried to smile, but tears gathered in her eyes.

"She'll be okay," he said. It was a wish, he told himself, not a lie. He touched her knee to reassure her. Her skin was soft under his hand.

"You don't know that." Chloe still hadn't taken a bite from her sandwich.

"She's in the best hands. Jeff's a good vet. He'll take good care of her."

Chloe nodded. "If only I'd pulled her back farther when I saw the truck coming ..."

"Chloe—" he paused until she looked at him, "—this isn't your fault."

She glanced down, slumping. She still held the sandwich in her lap. He'd finished his, so he drew her into an embrace. She didn't resist. Instead, she laid her head on his shoulder and tucked her feet up beside her.

He stroked her back in silence and wished like hell there was something more that he could do. A few minutes later, she started nibbling at her sandwich. One small victory.

When she finished, she sighed and pulled away. "I guess you need to get home."

He shook his head. "I'm here. I'll stay with you—I mean, I don't mean ... I ..." He took a breath. "I mean that I'll stay here, on the couch, tonight. I know you are worried so I'm not going anywhere."

"I know I should insist you go, but I won't. Not tonight." She leaned into him again.

"Good." So they stayed on the couch with his arm over her

shoulders.

"Thank you. I don't know what I would have done without you today."

"Any time." He meant what he said. He wished he could scrub away all her hurt, but settled for squeezing her tighter. After a few long, silent minutes, he felt her body loosen under his touch.

"Do you want to watch a movie?"

"Sounds great," he said.

They found an old romantic comedy neither of them had seen—well, truth be told, he hadn't watched a movie like that since his sister had left home years earlier. Halfway through, Chloe fell asleep in his arms, emotionally exhausted from the day. He pressed a kiss to the top of her head.

CHAPTER 7

The morning sunlight streamed into the living room, heating the small room. Considering how stifling the weather had been over the last few days, this wasn't surprising. Then again, it could be that she was within the embrace of a man who'd haunted her since high school.

And it felt pretty damn nice.

Well, except that she was scared to shake out the hand that had fallen asleep, in case she woke him.

It'd been years since Christopher had held her. Years.

Even in their big king-sized bed, which he'd abandoned long ago, they hardly touched. Whereas this moment was all about Luke's body pressed against hers in the most delicious way. Having a day bed as a couch had its benefits.

But how could she have slept like this? Plastered against him. And when did he lie behind her to spoon her?

Luke was a friend. He'd stayed the night to console her. It'd been perfectly platonic and yet here she was with her butt all cozy with his crotch. Chloe's heart raced. She could feel the outline of his equipment below the belt, causing all kinds of crazy thoughts to fill her head.

She really needed to choose different reading material before she went to bed at night. Lately her e-reader had been filled with all sorts of naughty, and that was clearly having an impact on her reaction to Luke.

Well, no, it wasn't.

Truth be told, Luke had always had a presence in her mind and her heart. Ever since he said she was perfect when they were under a car in shop class. The class had been her dad's idea, and she'd hated it. Especially when Amy Brewster had whispered loud enough for the whole class to hear that Chloe would be too fat to fit under the car.

It was weird because at the time she hadn't thought she was particularly fat. Thinking back, she had probably been wrong. Christopher had helped her see that. Of course, she still could have done without the treadmill.

Her fingers tingled to the point of pain.

Chloe inched her hand away from where it tucked up awkwardly under her head and tried to dangle it over the edge of the cushion.

Luke's arm tightened around her. His hand was strategically located along her lower ribcage—all in all, a pretty safe place, bulge-wise.

Her fingers were really painful now as the blood rushed back in.

Gah, she couldn't stand it.

She eased out of Luke's hold and sat up. She rubbed her prickling hand.

"What's the matter?"

Luke's voice suggested he had been awake for a while. It was sweet that he had just held her. She couldn't remember anyone doing that before.

"Pins and needles in my hand." She smiled apologetically at him.

Lines marked his face from where he'd lain against the corduroy pillow. She itched to smooth his disheveled hair into place, but that seemed a little too intimate. All things considered, that was a strange line to draw in the sand, but it was her line.

Luke didn't bother to sit up, and she wondered if she should move to the other chair now that they were both awake. She didn't want to.

Luke smiled. "Here," He reached for her hand and she placed it in his much larger one.

His chest was only a few inches away, and she really wanted to bend over and touch it with her cheek. But what would he think? Last night when he'd held her, it'd felt different because he'd been consoling her. Today, if she cuddled up to his muscular chest, it'd be ... well ... for entirely other reasons.

He rubbed the muscles and kneaded the tingles away. His fingers were magic. What would his hands feel like on the rest of her body?

She stared into his eyes, barely registering that she was leaning toward him. Closer to him.

She was going to smooch with Luke Larsen.

The phone rang and she yanked from his grasp. She blinked at him. Her ring tone sang through the room again and she scrambled for her purse. She pulled out the cell phone and her heart thundered when she saw it was the vet's office.

"Yes? Hello?" She didn't wait for an answer or any pleasantries. "Is everything okay with Ginger?"

"Ms. Wagner? I'm calling about Ginger."

She glanced at Luke, who had come to stand beside her. His eyes narrowed, waiting for some indication from her on Ginger's status.

"Is she okay?"

"Yes, the doctor has examined her this morning and says you can pick her up any time today."

"Oh, thank God!" She gave a thumbs-up to Luke, whose face relaxed at the news.

They made arrangements, then Chloe hung up the phone.

"That's great, Chloe," Luke said.

Chloe bounced. "It's fantastic. Oh, God, I was so worried!" She hugged him on impulse. She had to do something with all the happiness spurting through her body. "I'm so ... Oh, you can't believe how relieved I am!"

He hugged her back.

And then she realized she and Luke were hugging. And that her arms weren't letting go. She leaned back and smiled at him. "Thank you for staying with me. It would have been a long night otherwise." She didn't know why, but her voice was soft. Like a whisper. But why would she be whispering to Luke?

"You're welcome." Then his gaze drifted lower, over her face, until it landed on her mouth.

The impulse to kiss him kicked into gear again.

She opened her mouth. And he tightened his arms around her, pulling her closer to him. Body against body.

His lips brushed with tantalizing delicacy against hers. His hands spread over her back. When his fingers found a sliver of exposed skin at the hem of her shirt, he didn't stop. He drew enticing, teasing circles on that little bit of flesh.

Her hands gripped his strong back, fisting into the worn fabric of his shirt. Someone—it could have been her—moaned.

His tongue traced her lips and she opened wider for him. Man alive, he knew how to make a girl want more. The firm pressure of his hard chest against her breasts was so enticing. She wanted to escalate their embrace, by at least another bazillion notches.

She played with his buttons until they came free. She shoved the shirt from his body and his muscular flesh was available to her. She molded her hands to the contours of his body and her own flushed with need.

Luke was patient though. He explored her mouth with his. He kept his hand in perfectly safe places on her back, no matter how much she squirmed against him and pulled him closer.

Then she moaned—this time she knew it was her—and he moaned in response.

In that moment, something shifted in Luke. He spun her around and pressed her against the cool wall. His hot lean body came against her hard. His leg thrust between hers. One hand cradled her head, teasing the sensitive area along her neck.

He guided his other hand over her body until it arrived just below her breast. There he paused, as if unsure if he could be so bold. Breathlessly, she arched into him to urge him on.

When he cupped her breast, she whimpered. She grabbed his hips and held him against her as his finger rubbed her nipple until it was aroused and protruding through her T-shirt.

Was she really going to have sex with Luke this morning?

Hell yes.

She squirmed and he leaned back a little to give her space. She stared him in the eye, before pulling her T-shirt over her head and tossing it to the floor.

"You are beautiful," he murmured.

She smiled. When he said it like that, she could almost believe it. It was a lie that lovers said to one another, and that in itself was touching.

He bent to lay soft kisses along her neck. Then he made his way lower, down her collarbone to the crest of her breast.

When he closed his mouth around her nipple, she grabbed his head.

This was crazy. She'd never grabbed Christopher that way. Never. Not once.

What was going on with her?

She blinked and glanced down at him. His silky hair slipped through her fingers, but the sight of his face pressed to her round breast made her weak at the knees. His tanned skin was so dark against her pale skin and—

Good grief, from this angle her breast appeared as big as his head.

She caught their reflection in the mirror over the kitchen table and saw her other breast in his grasp, all droopy, and spilling over his long fingers. God, her boob was bigger than his hand. And look at the bulge springing out from the top of her pyjama pants.

Christopher was right. She was a fat cow.

She dropped her hands from Luke's head, and they landed on his wide shoulders. Why did the man have to be a god? If he were balding or had a paunch, she wouldn't feel so unsuitable for him.

"What's wrong?" Luke's words fanned over her heated skin. When she didn't answer, he straightened. "What's wrong?"

She closed her eyes—mortified by what she'd seen in the mirror. How could she tell him he deserved better?

"I'm sorry. I'm—" *Such a heifer.* She bit her lip.

"Hey, don't be sorry." He brushed his lips over her forehead. "I think I rushed you. I'm the one who is sorry."

She couldn't look at him. He dropped a kiss to her temple. Then he pulled her into a hug—a perfectly platonic hug. Well, except for the fact that she was topless, and he was topless, and their nipples were mingling.

"You've been through a scare. I didn't mean to take advantage."

"I'm sorry, Luke. It has nothing to do with you. I'm ..." What? A loser? Why couldn't she be that carefree kid she'd been in high school?

She took a ragged breath and then he loosened his hold and stepped back. Chloe crossed her arms, covering as many bumps as she could.

"I'm sorry ... I shouldn't have ..." She shook her head. And laughed. "Well, you know ..."

Luke smiled at her. His eyes were soft with understanding. "I can wait."

"Don't say that." Chloe swallowed. "Don't wait for me, Luke. You need to find someone pretty, perfect for you ..."

He scowled. "You are all of those things."

She rolled her eyes. "You don't have to say that to me. We're better friends than that, aren't we?"

His eyebrows knit together. "What are you talking about? Does this have to do with that idiot you used to live with?"

"Christopher was right, Luke. I am fat. I am—"

"Stop, okay?" He held up his hand to arrest her words. "He was a fucking ... Never mind. He doesn't deserve for us to spend time even thinking about him. He was wrong. I'm telling you that you are beautiful because you are. Always have been. "

Chloe pursed her lips. "You don't have to—"

His finger covered her mouth. "I'm not saying anything I don't believe. Okay?" She stared at him. He nodded, as if encouraging her to agree with him. "Chloe?"

She nodded meekly. "Okay." But she knew it was a lie.

He shook his head at her feeble response. "You'll see," he said. He squeezed her hand. "But in the meantime, I have to get back to the house and you need to collect your puppy. I'll see you later?"

"Um, sure. Later." But even as she said it, she feared they'd never really recover from this. Why did she have to kiss him today? Their friendship had been going so well. And now everything was all messed up.

Just like her.

CHAPTER 8

It'd been over a day since she'd woken in Luke's arms. She'd had a fitful sleep in her own bed, between checking on Ginger every hour or so, and missing Luke's warmth and strength to calm her.

It'd given her a lot of time to think.

In the moment she'd withdrawn from Luke, she'd made an excuse to herself that she didn't want to hurt him with a rebound relationship, but that was a lie. She wasn't so distraught about ending things with Christopher that she was in need of a rebound. The truth was she'd checked out of her other relationship long ago. It'd just taken longer for her to actually pack her belongings.

They hadn't been intimate for years. They slept in separate bedrooms, presumably because of his snoring. And he kept telling her she was fat and undesirable.

And she had believed him.

None of those things had made her love grow strong.

Chloe sighed. Was she just making up reasons to get involved with Luke?

The air was heavy with humidity. Dark clouds crowded over the sky, making a storm imminent. The expectation of it was palpable.

There was no way she and Ginger were going on a long walk tonight, even through the fields. And they certainly wouldn't be on the road any time soon. The accident was too fresh.

Ginger bumped the door handle with her nose.

"We're just going for a quick stop in the yard, right? " Chloe said to Ginger as she opened the door. "Then we'll snuggle on the couch and watch TV."

Ginger wiggled her tail and went outside.

"Hurry, before the rain starts."

The dog walked through the garden, sniffing at every flower and every blade of grass.

The evening was eerily quiet, as if all the other creatures were already taking cover.

"Go on," Chloe encouraged as she trailed behind Ginger. "Go to the bathroom, then we can go back inside."

Big, fat raindrops smacked against the ground.

"Come on, sweetheart, the sooner you—" Her words were obliterated by a sizzling crack of lightning, followed by a loud crash of thunder. Shit. Was the house hit?

Not seeing any immediate flames or smoke, Chloe's panic subsided. She and Ginger needed to get inside.

Where was Ginger?

She had vanished.

Lightning scorched the air again, illuminating the yard. Ginger's backside was hightailing it down the driveway and around the shrub hedge on the edge of the property. This time, a heartbeat passed before the corresponding thunder rumbled overhead. Chloe's heart jumped.

"Ginger, stop!" Chloe sprinted after her, but Ginger kept running. Shit, what should she do? Her aunt had a dog once that always ran to the nearest culvert for shelter. It was a stupid spot to hide, given the amount of rain that could fall in an Alberta storm, but dogs probably didn't think about that too much.

Chloe ran up the road. Water was already pooling in the ditch's low spot. Was Ginger already in the culvert? The grassy slope was slick, so Chloe travelled most of the incline on her butt. Her hands were muddy. Her clothes were soaked. And she prayed Ginger was there, so they could go back home.

"Ginger, come on out."

The narrow hole was dark. It was impossible to see if the dog was in there or not.

She was staring through the culvert when another arc of lightning crossed the sky and lit up the air. No Ginger.

Shit.

How far would she run? She had to stop soon, right? At least there was a bigger space between the lightning and thunder now, so the storm was drawing away.

When Chloe arrived at the corner, Ginger was still missing in action.

The electrical storm danced all around, but the thunder's rumbling sounded more like a hungry belly than a bomb. Hopefully the storm wouldn't roll back again. But if it did? She was the tallest thing around. She could attract the lightning herself.

This was probably really stupid.

The next round of thunder and lightning were closer together. Shit. She had to get out of the storm. Running through the prairies in the middle of an electrical storm had to be one of the dumbest things she'd ever done.

Luke's lights were on. Thank God.

Chloe knocked on the door. No answer. She banged harder.

Finally a shadow crossed by the window and he opened the door. "Jesus, Chloe, what's happened?" He ushered her inside.

"Is Ginger here?"

He brushed his jeans with his hands, leaving white streaks across the denim. Was that flour? "No, I haven't seen her. Is she lost?"

Then a flash of orange bolted through the open door and into the house.

"Ginger! Oh, thank God you are okay. I was so worried." Chloe rushed over and hugged Ginger. Her plastic cone was splattered with mud, her coat was soaked, and she was the most incredible sight Chloe had ever seen. Wet dog smell be damned, she never wanted to let Ginger go.

Luke shut the door behind them, then disappeared. A moment later, he returned with a handful of towels, which he tossed toward them. He grinned and shook his head. "You two are a mess."

Chloe started with Ginger, patting her fur and wiping her feet. She checked the bandage, but it seemed to have survived the mad dash through the countryside without problem. Then Chloe rubbed the other towel through her own hair and wiped her arms and legs. She had more mud on her than Ginger. She'd feel a lot better if she went home and had a bath.

"I'm sorry to be such a bother, but can you drive us home?"

"I can in a bit, but I have a few things on timers and can't—" As if on cue, a loud repetitive beep called from the kitchen. "I need to get that."

She nodded, since he seemed to be waiting for her okay, and he left to tend to whatever he was making. Alone on the porch, Chloe closed her eyes for a moment as her heart rate geared down. Thank God Ginger was safe. That dog would give her a heart attack yet.

After a deep breath, Chloe patted the towel over her soaked clothes.

Oh, God, she was wearing Luke's T-shirt. The one he had thrown away. She'd salvaged it from the garbage and washed it. She'd liked having something of his, even though she wondered if that made her pathetic, desperate or a stalker. And now he would realize what she'd done.

She eased out of her mud-caked shoes and pulled off her sopping wet socks. Then there wasn't anything else to do but go see Luke and hope he wouldn't recognize the plain black T-shirt as his.

"Wow, what smells so good?" She looked around. The place had been completely renovated since she'd been there last. Had Luke done all that? The wall between the kitchen and the living room was gone and had been replaced by a wide island. The fireplace, where Ginger was already settled, had been resurfaced with slate.

Ginger's paw rested on Jasper, who opened his eyes long enough to see who had joined him. The cat, curled in a ball on the sofa, twitched its tail twice and then covered its face with its paw.

Chloe crossed the room and sat on a stool by the island.

Luke set the timer on the stove, then a second timer beside a tray of cookies.

"You made these? I'm impressed."

Luke shrugged. "My grandfather was a baker before immigrating. He thought all the men in the family needed to know how to bake, so when other boys were out fishing with their grandfathers, I was learning how to knead bread." He laughed.

The sound warmed her and she almost forgot about her chilled clothes for a moment. As far as kitchens went, the finishes—granite, dark wood and stainless steel— were as masculine as she could imagine and perfectly suited to a strong sexy cowboy. He was obviously comfortable here.

"Why two timers?"

"If you leave the cookies on the tray too long they harden, but if you take them off too fast, they wilt. I don't really need the second timer for the cookies on the tray, but it is a habit and it reminds me of our lessons." He glanced away then, as if embarrassed.

"I don't have any memories like that of my grandparents. They all live in Ontario."

"I miss him."

"I'm sorry," she said. She wanted to comfort him, but words seemed inadequate.

He nodded his acknowledgement of her condolences. Then he leaned back against the counter and crossed his arms, as if studying her and not sure what to make of their situation.

She shifted on her seat. The last time they'd seen one another, neither of them had shirts on. Then her body erupted into a giant shiver—whether because of the memory or her damp clothing—releasing a fresh bout of wet dog smell.

"Listen, why don't you take off your soaked clothing, since I'll probably be an hour or so. I can pop them in the dryer, then drive you back later."

"No, I'm fine—" But her words were pointless as another shiver rippled over her. "Oh, shit, I'm getting mud all over your stool, aren't I?"

Luke rolled his eyes at her, as if mud was the least of his worries, then he left her in the kitchen again. God, those cookies smelled great. She crossed to the cooling tray and breathed in the mouth-watering aroma of melted chocolate and the yumminess of freshly baked cookies.

"Try one," Luke said behind her.

Chloe jumped. "You scared me."

"Go ahead." He nodded to the tray.

She was tempted, but Christopher's voice chimed through the back of her head.

Luke smiled at her. "You know you want to."

Chloe grabbed a cookie. The first bite was heavenly. She closed her eyes and let the soft chocolate chips slide over her tongue. She moaned with happiness. This was why she never baked. She'd eat them all before they'd even cooled. When she opened her eyes, Luke leaned toward her. His eyes were dark and he was staring at her mouth again.

"This cookie is amazing," she said.

Her words made him blink. "I'm glad you approve." His voice was deeper than normal, and the timbre of it sent a new ripple over her. This one had nothing to do with the state of her clothing.

"Here is a housecoat." He shoved a big terry cloth garment at her.

Chloe stared at it. Outside the wind howled, sending the rain slamming against the windowpanes.

"I've only worn it once. It was Christmas morning, right after my mom gave it to me. So it's fine. It's clean." He thrust it at her again, and this time she took it.

"Um, thanks," she said. "Where should I change?"

CHAPTER 9

After Chloe left the room, Luke let out a deep breath. Ever since he left her house the day before, he had convinced himself he'd messed up royally by kissing her. He'd gone too fast. But he didn't regret it. It had been, in one word, amazing. Then when she showed up wearing the T-shirt he'd left at her place, he was envious of that bit of cotton for how it clung to her body.

He had to quit thinking about that.

But it didn't help that he could hear the shower in the bathroom. *Get a grip.* He studied the storm through the window. He counted the seconds between the flash of lightning and the boom of thunder, and tried to forget that Chloe was naked down the hall.

She had come to him and that gave him the opportunity to make things right between them again. But that would only happen if he could keep his cool.

But maybe the time for keeping his cool had passed. Maybe it was time to reveal to Chloe how much he loved her, show her how happy he could make her—

One of his timers buzzed.

He scooped the cookies off the cooled tray with a metal lifter and placed them in a tin container. He'd planned to make another couple dozen for his nephew's bake sale, but his plans had changed when two waterlogged visitors crashed his house. Then again, he'd planned to bake them a few of days ago, but after he'd spent the night at Chloe's, following the accident, he'd had to buy all new ingredients. Somehow eggs and milk that had sat out in the sweltering heat weren't too appealing.

He was on the last cookie when Chloe cleared her throat behind him.

He turned with the cookie balanced on the spatula, then he forgot what he was doing. The bulky terry cloth robe did something spectacular to Chloe's figure.

He had thought terry cloth would be safe. Innocent.

He'd been wrong.

The material accentuated her luscious curves, and the tie cinched tight around her narrow waist. If that wasn't bad enough, the purple, silky strap of a bra poked out from the middle of her folded pile of wet clothes. She was naked under the robe.

Dammit, now he was envious of his robe, too.

She gasped and looked down. "Oh, you broke it."

He followed her gaze. The forgotten cookie had fallen off his lifter to the floor. He crouched to pick up the pieces, thankful to have something else to do besides stare at her. "Do you want to throw those clothes in the washer? It is down the hall beside the bathroom."

A moment later he heard the hiss of water filling the washing machine over the sounds of the storm. When she returned this time, he was prepared. His hands were empty and the cookies were safe.

She climbed onto the stool again and leaned forward, creating a tempting gap in the neckline of the robe. He propped himself against the far counter with his thumbs hooked into the belt loops on his jeans.

Nope, that wasn't going to work. After reading some book on body language, his sister had teased him incessantly that by doing that he was pointing at his goods in a *hey, check me out* gesture.

He crossed his arms over his chest again.

"When I got in there, I realized the mud had soaked through, so I had a shower. I hope you don't mind."

A vision of what he thought she'd look like in his bathroom flashed through his mind. He swallowed. "Feel better now?"

She smiled and nodded. "Is there anything I can do to help?"

If his intention had been to flirt, he would have had a dozen responses to that question. But this was Chloe and he wanted more. "Everything is under control. There is one more tray of cookies, then I'm done for the night."

"Can I help with the dishes?"

"Nope, I did them as I went."

She looked disappointed. True, he supposed he wasn't being very conversational. Maybe because all he could think about was how he wanted to pull her close again.

"Do you always make cookies in the rain?"

He smiled and shook his head. "My nephew Jeremy needs them for a bake sale. Everyone knows my sister can't bake, so he asked me. I'm going to take them over to his house tomorrow morning. The school bus comes at eight." She wouldn't care when the bus came, but he couldn't stop himself from calculating how much time he would have with her if she decided to stay the night.

Not that she was. Nope. After his last batch was out of the oven, he would drive her home and that'd be the end of all the crazy thoughts going through his head. He needed to slow down and court her. At least he'd learned *something* from their heated embrace in her kitchen.

"You know, I've been meaning to ask you something for a while."

"Oh?"

"Why do you always walk this way, I mean, not that I mind—" he winked, "—but I was curious why you haven't gone up to the woods or down by the wetland."

Chloe tilted her head. "I heard they were dangerous, and I didn't want to put Ginger at risk."

"Dangerous?" He laughed. "Who told you that?"

"Helen Trent. She talked about badgers and coyotes and ..." A blush stole over her face. "Was that not true?"

Luke shook his head. "I suppose there have been some animals around now and again, but I haven't seen any for a few years."

"She lied?"

He grinned, thinking about the day he'd seen the same old woman in the post office. "I think she was trying to get us together."

She frowned. "Devin's single, isn't he? People should only try to match make with their own children."

Luke glanced at the timer. Still a few minutes to go. "I don't know if Devin's ready for that yet." The former cowboy had closed himself off from the world since his wife had died, but Luke didn't want to talk about that tonight.

Chloe shook her head. "I think Ginger was trying to get us together, too." She laughed. "Even tonight she had to bring me over here in a storm." She crossed her arms over her chest. "But I'm glad we are *friends*."

He didn't believe her. Not for a minute.

"It'll be a few minutes for the last batch. We could go sit by the fire."

"Sounds like a plan." She smiled.

He loved when he could make her smile.

She sat on the edge of the ottoman in front of the hearth, and adjusted the seam in the robe to cover her legs. But it was too late. He'd already seen more of her creamy, smooth skin than he ever had before. He grabbed a couple of cookies and joined her in the living room.

"The storm is wild out there, isn't it?" She peered out the window.

"I think it is circling back." He handed her a cookie. "You could sit on the sofa."

"Oh, no." She glanced at Odie. "I couldn't disturb the cat." Then she considered the treat in her hand. "I don't want to eat them all. Jeremy will have nothing to take."

"The cook and his assistant have to sample for quality control." Now that he knew how erotic a chocolate chip cookie could be, he wanted to watch her enjoy another one. Before tonight he would have sworn that both the cookie and the terry cloth were innocent, safe. But not with Chloe.

"Excellent, because they are spectacular and I was dying for another taste." She laughed. She tapped her cookie to his, as if they were wine glasses. He bit into his when she bit into hers, but had to remind himself to chew as she closed her eyes to savor the taste. Would she moan like that when he tasted her? He really wanted to know. Her skin was growing pink, probably from the heat of the fire, but he itched to know how far that blush crept.

When she licked the melted chocolate from her fingers and grinned at him, he knew she had no idea what she was doing to him. Was that better or worse than if she did? He wasn't sure.

The timer went off again and he escaped to the kitchen for a moment.

He lifted the cookies off the hot tray, without waiting this time, unusually eager to be finished baking tonight. If he'd had any more trays to stick in the oven, he'd probably have burned them.

"Well, that's it," he said when he returned to the living room. "I'm done. I can drive you home now." This was her moment to reinforce that whole *friend* idea.

"My clothes won't be ready yet."

"It's up to you. I can lend you my robe if you want to get out of here. Or we can hang out for a bit."

"I'm happy to wait. Don't let me disrupt your plans."

He sat down beside her. Thank God she didn't want to leave. "How did you get chocolate ..." He reached up to clear away a bit of chocolate from her cheek. Just the other day he'd wiped away ice cream, and now some cookie ... He'd have to stay close when she ate if there were going to be opportunities to touch her.

When she stared at his hand, he slowed his action. His fingers skimmed her smooth skin. He hadn't meant for the touch to be so intimate, but now that he'd touched her he wanted to continue. Her mouth opened a little as her gaze drifted down his face to his lips.

In that moment, he wanted to tell her he loved her. He'd held it in for so damned long. He leaned forward. As he neared her, he whispered, "You are so beautiful."

She stiffened and turned away. "You shouldn't say things like that, Luke."

He dropped his hand and retreated to his favorite chair. When would she ever believe him? "I don't say things I don't mean."

She stood and walked to the fireplace, carefully stepping over the dogs, withdrawing even further from him.

"What's wrong with saying you're beautiful?"

"We both know I'm not." Her voice was soft, barely audible above the storm and the crackle of the fire. She drew in a ragged breath.

Shit, she was going to cry. What the hell? What woman cried when she was given a compliment?

Particularly when it was the truth.

He wished she would face him, but he didn't want to pressure her. So he studied the way her drying hair curled along the robe's collar. After another rumble of thunder overhead, he thought she might turn around again.

She didn't. But at least her tears appeared to have subsided.

"I don't understand," he said, figuring it was best to be honest. "I've always known you're beautiful. Your hair is the color of wheat fields, your eyes match those blue flowers my mom used to grow, your body ... Well, your body is enough to make me ache. Thinking about you keeps me awake at night." He cleared his throat. "I'm sure there are more poetic ways to tell you that, but I don't really do poetry."

Chloe clutched the mantel of the fireplace, but stayed turned away. Well, that was his answer then.

"Listen, I don't know how you feel about me," he continued. "Given the other day when I kissed you and you freaked out, I'm gonna guess you aren't interested. I get that. It's okay." Luke leaned back in his chair. "But don't worry. You don't have to stand on the opposite side of the room from me all night. I can control myself."

Chloe turned to him. "What are you talking about?"

Luke took a deep breath. "We both know I like you. Hell, I've been half in love with you most of my life. I'm used to keeping it under wraps. I wanted to tell you, that's all. Tonight, in this storm, I wanted to tell you. Tomorrow, we can go back to the other way again."

Chloe marched to the ottoman and sat down in front of him. She leaned forward. "How could you love me? I'm a fat pig."

A tic on the side of his head started thrumming. "I understand you believe some things about yourself. I'm sorry that you do. But I get it. But don't question if I'm telling you the truth about how I feel. And I don't want you to ever call yourself that again. You are gorgeous and vibrant, and any man would be honored to have you in his life." He peered into her eyes, hoping he was making his point. "Honored," he repeated.

A soft "Oh" was all she said before she put her hand over her mouth, and then the tears that had threatened earlier began to fall.

Shit.

"Chloe." He knelt at her feet in the next heartbeat, wiping the wetness from her face. "None of that either, okay?"

When their gazes met, she blinked but didn't look away. His fingers swept over her cheek. He was through trying to convince her with words.

CHAPTER 10

The pounding storm, the sizzling fire, and the drone of the washing machine all faded under the hammering of Chloe's heart. Luke was going to kiss her again. And she wanted him to.

He had a way of making her feel pretty. Maybe because he really did seem to believe it.

How? She had no idea. But maybe it didn't matter. Maybe all that mattered was the way he was looking at her right now.

His intense gaze and soft touch were reassuring at the very least ... and thrilling. All the emotions and longing that had been left dangling from their last embrace clamored to life.

He moved in slowly, as if he was scared to spook her again. But this time there was no retreat. She wanted this as much as he did. Besides she'd given him enough opportunities to run away and he kept staying.

She leaned into him. The aroma of cookies clung to his skin, mixing intoxicatingly with his own masculine scent. And she wanted to taste him. Lick his body. Know him. Her gaze locked on his, as her hands skimmed down the hard planes of his chest. Grabbing his shirt, she yanked it from his jeans.

He grunted approval at her action. When he leaned back to give her more space, she followed him.

"Oh!"

She fell ignobly from the ottoman to the floor. The robe gaped open. Luke's gaze took in the expanse of skin in one sweep and she would have sworn he growled. "Come here," he said as he pulled her to her feet.

Then he swept her into his arms.

"Good grief," she said. "Put me down. I'm too f—"

He smothered her protest with his mouth. When he drew away, he narrowed his eyes as if to dare her to defy him again. Then he carried her down the hall as if she weighed no more than the terry cloth robe she was wrapped in.

She'd never been carried by a strong, muscular man before.

She liked it.

She glanced around the dark bedroom, curious about where he slept every night. She only had time to see that it had hardwood floors and big windows before he set her on the soft bed, crawled over her and covered her lips with his again.

The gentle control he'd shown in the living room was gone. His hard body pressed to hers, and she drew one leg up over his. He was still fully clothed, and the coarse denim scraped against her inner thigh deliciously.

She pulled at his shirt again, and the buttons gave way under her tugs. Then her hands were on him again. She murmured his name as she caressed the muscular planes of his body, wanting to know everything about him. He broke the kiss for a moment, and braced himself over her, giving her space to explore him.

"Tell me you are beautiful," he said when she met his gaze.

She shook her head. "Don't do this, not now."

"Do you think I want you?" He shifted so she couldn't deny his erection against her leg.

She swallowed. "Yes."

"Do you think I think you are beautiful?"

She glanced away.

"Chloe, look at me." He waited until she peered up at him again. "Tell me."

"Yes, I think you think I'm beautiful."

"Never doubt it," he whispered. His breath fanned across her cheek. His voice was deep with want. He bent close, until his lips touched her ear. "I don't lie."

Her breath caught at his words.

"I want to see you, Chloe. I want to turn on that little light beside my bed so I can—"

She stiffened and tried to draw him down to her again, to make him forget that ridiculous idea. He nuzzled her neck for a moment, eliciting a soft moan from her, before lifting away from her.

"Don't worry, darlin', I have a heap of kisses waiting for you, but I want to see you. I want to see your beauty. Will you let me?"

This was mortifying.

He would see her bulges, her dimpled skin, her cellulite. Could she really do this?

He wanted it. He'd know what he was getting that way. Panicked sweat sprang over her. Her chest ached. Then she nodded.

"I know that was hard for you," he said. "Thank you for trusting me." Relief shone through his smile. As soon as his back was turned, she grabbed the robe closed again, tight over her body, fisting the material in her hands.

With one tiny click, the room was bathed in a weak yellowy light that would be abhorrent to read by.

Still, she inched away from its meager glow—as if two inches would make any difference.

Luke stood by the bed then and looked down at her. His shirt hung loose over his chest, and his jeans couldn't disguise his hard desire. He was the sexiest man she'd ever seen. He stared into her eyes, perhaps aware that if he glanced at her body she might crawl farther away and end up falling off the edge of the bed.

He tossed his shirt from his body, revealing the wide strong breadth of his shoulders. When his hands came to rest on his belt buckle, she couldn't keep his gaze. Her attention was drawn to the slow deliberate way he removed the leather strap from its latch, uncovering the button of his jeans. Her pulse raced. She licked her lips as he slipped the button free and unfastened the zipper.

Her fingers twitched.

He shoved his jeans and boxers down, and she saw him.

She glanced at his face again. His hooded eyes were dark with desire, as if it turned him on to have her see him. He kicked his clothing aside and climbed onto the bed again.

Her breath was coming faster. Would he think she was going to strip for him, too?

Instead he stretched out beside her, putting his body between her and the feeble lamp light. The faint shadow he'd created eased a tiny percentage of her anxiety.

He propped himself up on one arm, and he reached for her with his other. He never let his gaze stray from her face, even as he glided his hand over her cheek, pulling his thumb across her lips, then lower, down her neck. She tingled with anticipation.

When his finger skated under the collar of the robe, she took a sharp intake of breath. He traced her collarbone with his finger. The robe opened a little wider with each tiny exploration. Her body rejoiced and her grip loosened. More of the fabric was nudged aside, but she didn't let go.

His callused fingers then traveled lower, between her breasts. Then he placed his hand against her chest, over her heart, as if to gauge her reaction by the rhythm of her heartbeats. Then he took a deep breath. Oddly, that calmed her.

"You need to let go if you want me to touch you more," he said. His large, strong hand covered hers, where they still clung to the robe. His heat soothed the tension in her fists.

"Let go," she repeated. That's what this was, wasn't it? Letting go. As she exhaled, she let her hands drop to the bed.

He rested his hand on the knotted tie for a moment, as if waiting for her protest, then tugged at it. With that gone, there would be nothing left to hold the cloth in place. Her heart hammered. The knot loosened quickly, as if eager to give up her secrets.

"You are stunning," he murmured as he slid his hand through the opening in her robe.

He hadn't seen what lay beneath the terry cloth yet, so she had to disagree. "You haven't even looked at me."

"Darlin', I haven't stopped looking at you." As he kissed her, he removed the robe and exposed her skin to the cool air of the night.

He brushed his thumb over her hardened nipples and she arched against him. Then he circled them leisurely with his forefinger. A wave of heat swept over her. But he didn't stay there. No, his hand drifted, playing over her rounded stomach as it progressed lower. When his exploration stopped at her hip, he drew his gaze from her eyes, tracing the same path. She grabbed the sheets to resist the urge to cover herself.

He hummed his appreciation at what he saw. But she could really believe that?

Sex would be so much easier if she could stay clothed through it. She hadn't been this apprehensive about being with a man since her first time. And that was ages ago. Why was it like this with Luke?

But she knew why. She'd come to care for him. She couldn't stand the idea of disappointing him.

Who was she kidding? She'd always had a soft spot in her heart for Luke. And since returning to Morning Lake, that spot had blossomed into something more intense and important. Could she love him? Was that why this was so critical?

She reached for him. Her panic subsided when he trembled under her touch.

She'd never felt so grounded by another person.

He pulled his leg over her newly bared one. Flesh against flesh.

She couldn't resist. She opened her legs, ever so slightly.

Seeing the invitation she offered, he pushed between her legs. His body shook as he found her core. He pressed his face into her shoulder as his fingers discovered her. His breathing was harsh and fast.

She'd done that to him.

He whispered her name over and over, with each stroke of his fingers against her. She moaned and her hips followed his rhythm.

"Tell me you are beautiful," he said.

"I'm beautiful," she replied. And for the first time she meant it. He'd done that to her. Even in her muddled, sexually addled brain, she finally understood. She hadn't needed to be skinny, she'd simply needed to find a real man ... The right man.

As his tongue played along her neck, right at the spot that sent tingling ripples across her, he removed the last bit of her robe.

Luke rose up beside her then. His eyes locked on her for one long moment, before his gaze drifted over her again.

"Beautiful," he murmured.

Then he grabbed a packet from his bedside table.

"You have protection?"

He grinned as he torn the wrapper open. "I was hopeful."

As he unrolled the condom over his erection, Chloe knew this wasn't a one-night thing for either of them. She quivered at the realization.

He positioned himself between her legs and knelt there for a moment. There was no shadow this time. The lamp shed light over her and she didn't try to hide from him.

When he leaned over her, he peered into her eyes. "I love you, Chloe," he said.

He didn't wait for her to reply, but kissed her as he placed himself at her entrance. She raised her hips, opening herself wider for him. Then he pushed into her slowly. When he was fully inside her, he paused. She wrapped her legs around his hips and grabbed him closer. Her heart burst with the beauty of Luke joining with her. He wiped her new tears away.

"Luke, I—" But her words were lost as he rocked against her.

Even as his pace increased, he never broke eye contact with her. Heat coursed over her as his body stroked hers. Over and over.

Harder. Deeper. More.

When her climax rippled through her, she clung to him. Luke stiffened over her a moment later. His face tensed with his own release.

When his body eased, he kissed her again and rolled them, still joined, to their sides.

When their breathing slowly quieted, Chloe brushed her hand over his cheek. She held his face directly in front of hers, so she could study his reaction to what she was about to say.

"Luke, I love you, too. I just couldn't imagine how or why you'd ever want to be with me." She took a deep breath. "Are you sure?"

He turned his head and pressed his lips to her palm. "You never need to question it again. I'll tell you how beautiful you are every day, right after I tell you I love you."

CHAPTER 11

Epilogue

When was Luke coming back? She had half a mind to saddle up and go hunting for him. He had said he was going out to check on the cattle, but she had no idea where the herd might be.

Chloe paced the length of Luke's porch. She stopped and listened for him, but all she heard was the rumble of tractors in the fields. The tall cottonwoods around the yard were turning yellow as the days grew shorter, but they still hadn't dropped their leaves, so she couldn't see if he was returning. She jiggled her keys and contemplated her options. Her news was too good. She wanted to tell him now.

When Ginger and Jasper trotted into the yard and headed for the water bowl, Chloe raced down the steps. A moment later, Luke came into sight. He jumped down from his horse when she ran up to him. He smiled and opened his arms. She hugged him tight, loving the smell of man and horse. He was hot, sweaty, and oh so sexy.

"I gave you a key so you don't have to wait outside for me," he said.

When she leaned back to tell him her news, he seized the opportunity to kiss her, hard and passionately. Her body responded with instant heat, and she moaned. Her hands sought access to him, and then something pushed them and they stumbled.

They broke apart, and Luke shook his head. "Jesus, Mickey, can't I kiss a beautiful woman?"

The horse nudged his shoulder again.

Luke shrugged. "I guess he doesn't want to wait. What are you doing out here anyway? Not that I wouldn't mind that kind of greeting every time you see me." He grinned.

"You'll never guess what happened," Chloe said.

He had been gathering Mickey's reins when she'd spoken. At her words, he stilled for a moment, but when he looked at her he was smiling. "You heard back from one of your interviews, didn't you? I told you it'd all work out." He led the horse down the driveway and reached for her hand with his free one. "Tell me all about it."

Chloe skipped beside him; she couldn't help it. "I've been offered a permanent fulltime position. And I've already talked to Laura about finalizing Ginger's adoption."

He squeezed her hand. "That's fantastic." He was still smiling, but it didn't reach his eyes. "Where are you and the little fur ball going?"

She frowned. "I'm not going anywhere. Joanie decided she didn't want to come back to work after her mat leave. I'm staying right here."

Luke stopped walking then. "Here? You're staying in Morning Lake?"

"It is the only place I want to be."

He dropped the reins again. He hooted as he picked her up and swung her around.

"Luke." She laughed. "Put me down."

"I don't ever want to let you go," he said. When he finally set her on her feet again, he knelt before her and held her hand in his. "Chloe Wagner, would you marry me?"

"Yes." Her heart raced and her eyes filled with tears. "Absolutely."

ONE LAST WORD
FROM HELEN TRENT

Outdoor weddings could be so unpredictable, but at least the weather had held out for this one. Helen Trent wasn't sure she'd have been able to stay very long if it'd rained and they were sent to the big white tents at the edge of the lawn. Her arthritis would have been such a bother.

But today the weatherman had been right, which was a good thing because Helen didn't want to miss a moment of the ceremony.

After all, she had to celebrate her success: Luke and Chloe were getting married because of her.

Helen sat back in her garden chair and smiled. Who would have guessed that matchmaking would be so easy? A little nudge here and there in spring blossomed to a wedding by fall. It was as easy as rhubarb crisp.

Wouldn't Charlie be surprised to find out she was a natural at this whole endeavor?

She'd asked Devin to bring her a little early. She'd said it was to make sure they had a place to park at the Larsen yard. She grinned. Little did he know that she was on the hunt for a bride for him. That boy—well, hardly a boy any longer—needed to get out and experience laughter and joy again. He wasn't going to do that while he was all cooped up in that old house of his.

She could almost see Charlie waggle his finger at her out the corner of her eye. She turned in the other direction.

Devin was standing off to the side with a few men. She recognized them all as neighbours. She pursed her lips. Where were the women, for heaven's sake?

She adjusted her hat, and looked around. There was Evie McEwen, Morning Lake's floral designer, fiddling with the rose arch. She bent to smell one of the flowers before securing it in place. A nice girl, but perhaps a bit too ... *something*. Helen couldn't put her finger on it, but Evie wasn't the right one for Devin.

There had to be someone else. Surely.

A pickup truck pulled into Luke's driveway and parked next to

Devin's. John Quinn hopped out and then crossed around the truck to help Rita Winston out of the cab. Those two went through the motions but anyone could see they weren't really interested in one another. Particularly John. Hmm ... that Rita was a beautiful woman. No. It didn't feel right either. Not for Devin.

Helen scratched her head.

This might take a while, but she didn't doubt for a moment that the right woman for Devin was out there. It was only a matter of time. She'd just have to keep an eye out. She would know the answer when she saw it.

THE END

TITLES BY LORRAINE PATON

Morning Lake Series:
Chloe's Matchmaking Terrier
Devin's Second Chance
Annie's Christmas Plan

ABOUT THE AUTHOR

When Lorraine Paton finished her master's degree, she was tempted to sign on to do a doctorate, but then she realized she wanted to write fiction more. So, by day, she works in a hectic office, and by night, she lets loose her passion for writing romance novels. She lives with two cats who hate one another and a wonderfully patient man with a sexy Scottish accent in Alberta, Canada, which is where her contemporary stories take place. A diehard romance reader and writer, her goal is to bring happily-ever-afters to as many people—*or characters*—as she can.

Connect with Lorraine on:
- her newsletter (http://eepurl.com/tYuqP)
- her blog (www.lorrainepaton.com),
- Twitter (twitter.com/patonlorraine), and
- Facebook (facebook.com/LorrainePaton.Author).